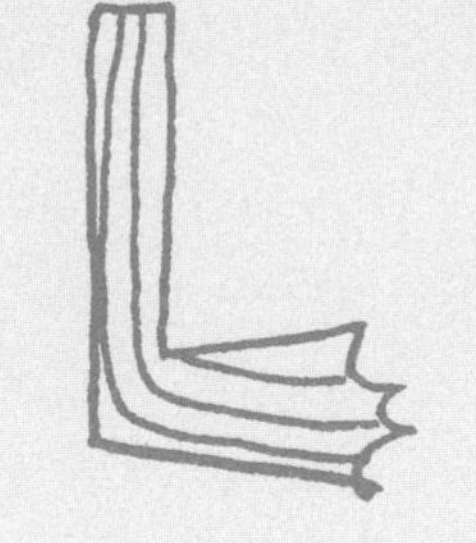

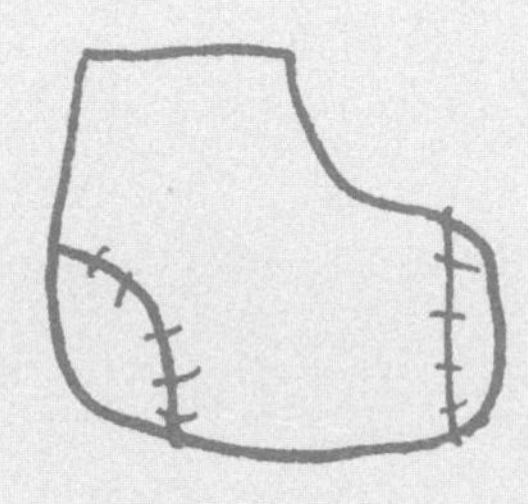
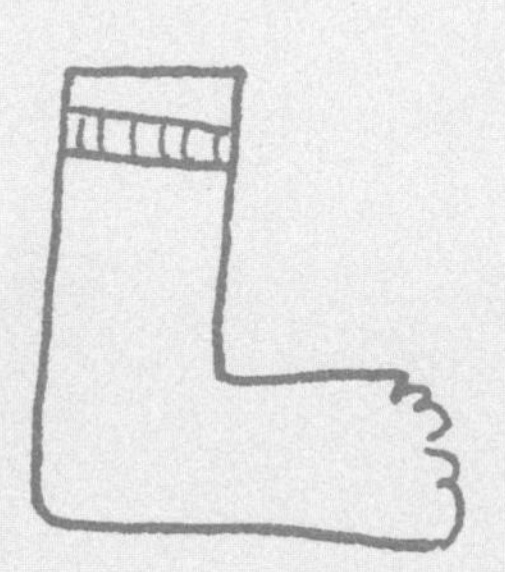

Socksquatch

So

cksquatch
Words and pictures by
Frank W. Dormer
Henry Holt and Company
NEW YORK

Flowers tremble.

Trees quake.

Socksquatch lumbers.

Socksquatch searches.

Got sock?
Foot cold.

Hi, Wayne!

No sock.

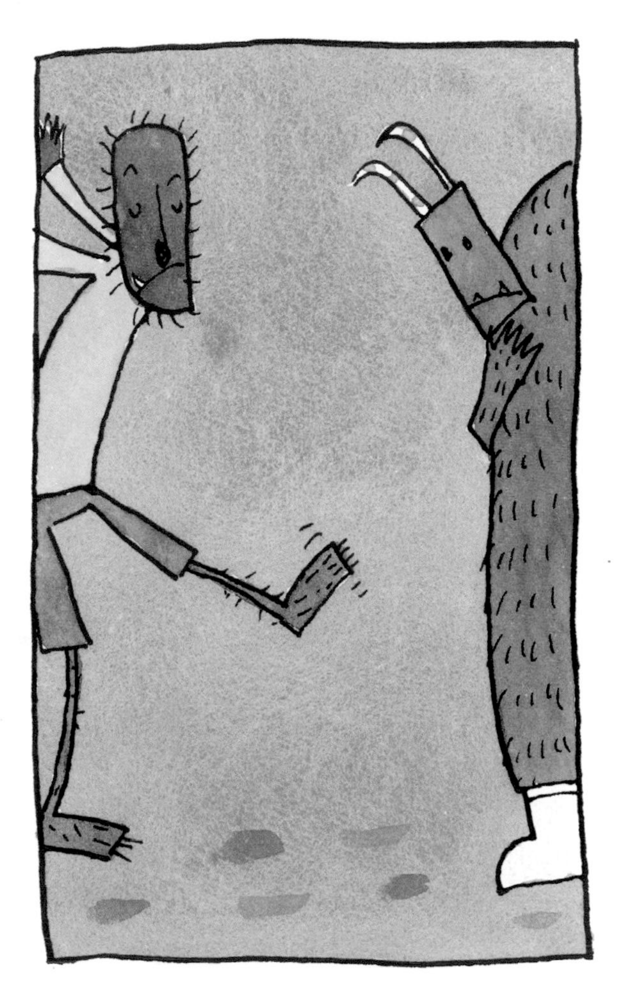

Just fur.

Here's Frank!

Got sock?

S-O-O-O-C-K.

Got sock.

Too **big**!

AAAA

Poor Socksquatch.

Martin hears.

AAAAAAAAA!

Martin comes.
Damsel comes too.

What
need?

Got sock?

No sock.

Just toes.

I do!

S-O-O-O-C-K.

Happy Socksquatch.

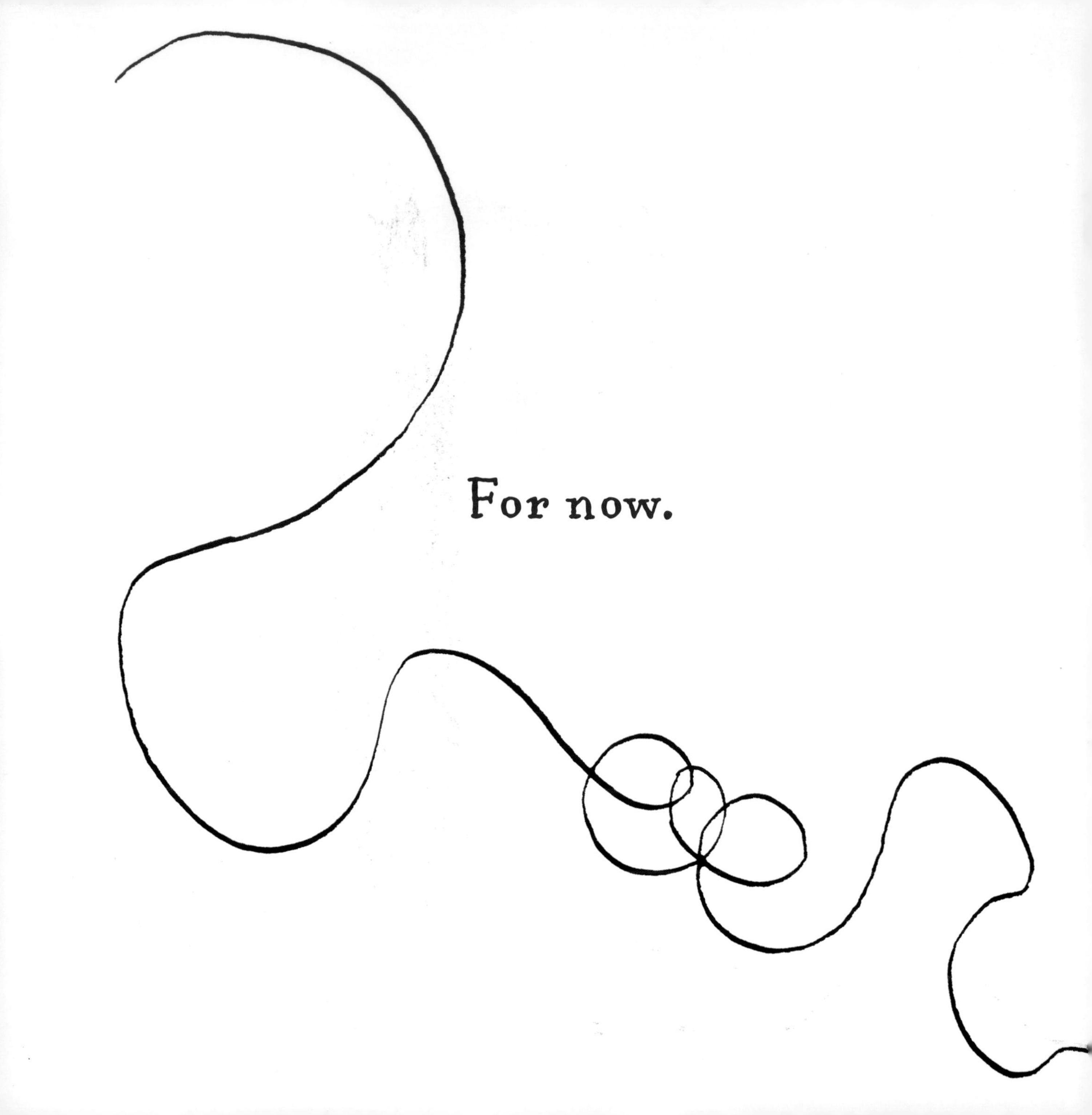

For now.

To Sockrateez,
finder of lost socks

Henry Holt and Company, LLC
Publishers since 1866
New York, New York 10010
www.HenryHoltKids.com

Distributed in Canada by H. B. Fenn and Company Ltd.

Library of Congress Cataloging-in-Publication Data
Dormer, Frank W.
Socksquatch / written and illustrated by Frank W. Dormer. – 1st ed.
p. cm.
Summary: Socksquatch tries to find a sock to warm his cold foot.
ISBN 978-0-8050-8952-3
[1. Monsters–Fiction.] I. Title.
PZ7.D72835o 2010 [E]–dc22 2009027413

First Edition–2010 / Designed by April Ward
Printed in June 2010 in China by Macmillan Production (Asia) Ltd.,
Kwun Tong, Kowloon, Hong Kong, on acid-free paper. ∞
Supplier Code: 10

1 3 5 7 9 10 8 6 4 2

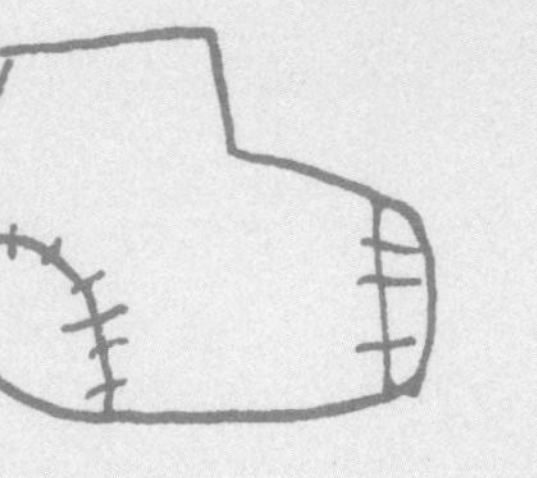

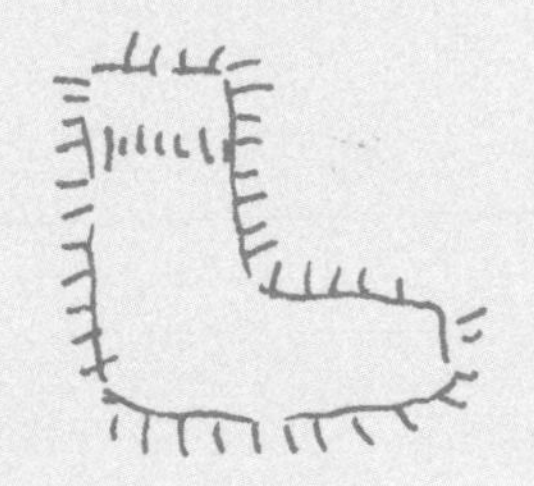
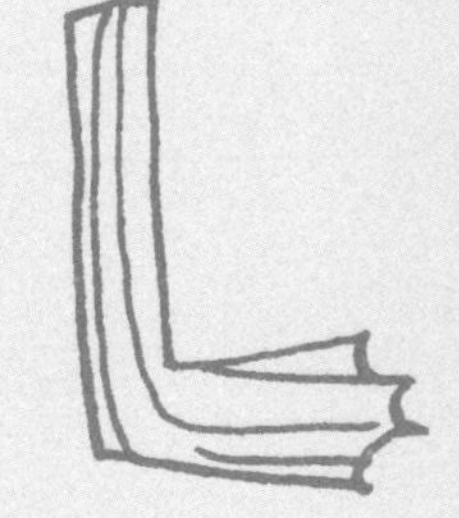
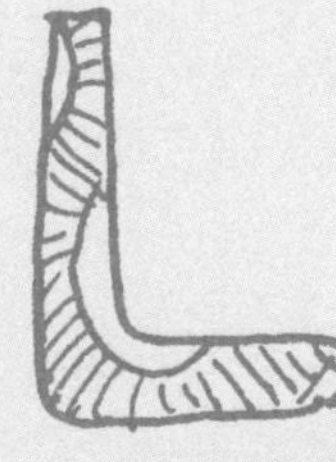

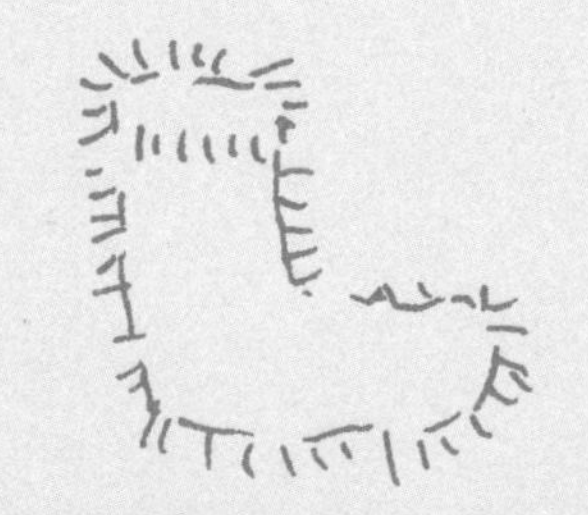